MW00885120

INSPIRATION AND DEDICATION

This story, years in the making, is inspired by and dedicated to my beloved Kyppa girl, an AKC Registered therapy dog and Canine Good Citizen. The sweetest, smartest, most beautiful dog that ever lived, you brought me more joy and happiness than I ever thought possible. I love you more every day.

Love, your proud Mumma

Copyright © 2015, Michelle Dube'. All rights reserved.

No portion of ther book can be reproduced or transmitted by any means without written permission from the author, except by reviewers who may quote brief excerpts and share the cover image in connection with reviews.
Author contact: fluff_2u@hotmail.com

Copyright © 2015, Illustrations by Shannon Sterner. All rights reserved.

Book Design by Conch Custom
Published with assistance from Conch Custom, an imprint of Nauset Press.
Publishing contact: info@nausetpress.com

ISBN-13: 978-1514601969
ISBN-10: 1514601966

Kyppa
and the
Duckling

By Fluff

Illustrations by Shannon Sterner

One lazy, hot afternoon, Kyppa followed her people down a winding path leading to a pond. She had been looking forward to a nap all day!

When they came to a sandy clearing, Kyppa plopped down with a sigh and fell fast asleep. Kyppa had just started to dream, when....

"Hey, wanna play?" asked a fluffy duckling. With a wrinkly forehead, Kyppa barked, "Woof! No! I just want to take a nap!"

"Please, please, *pleeeease, quack, quack, quack*," quacked the duckling with a tilt of her head.

Kyppa looked at the cute duckling and changed her mind, howling, "Arooooo! Oh, all right. What's your name?"

The duckling danced with excitement, "My name is Lily. What should we do?"

"Well," Kyppa said, "My name is Kyppa, and my favorite thing in the whole wide world is *runningggg*!!!" and she took off down the sandy beach! Kyppa has four long, skinny legs and she runs *very* fast!

Lily tried running and stumbled. She looked down at her big, floppy, webbed feet. Kyppa circled around and sprinted back to the duckling. "What's wrong?" she asked.

"You have four long, skinny legs and run very fast. But I have these big, floppy, webbed feet," said Lily.

"However, do you know what *webbed* feet are good for?" Lily said with excitement, "*swimmingggg*!!!!" The duckling then jumped into the pond with a splash and powered off on the surface of the water like a motor boat!

Kyppa quickly jumped in and doggy-paddled with her long, skinny legs. She didn't get very far before growing tired and turning back for shore.

The duckling circled around and swam back to Kyppa. "What's wrong?" she asked.

"Your big, floppy, webbed feet *are* awesome for swimming, but it turns out my long, skinny legs aren't so great for paddling in the water".

"I know," Kyppa shouted, "let's play tug of war!" Her eyes lit up as she spotted a big old branch on the sand. She grabbed it with her large mouth and teeth and dragged it around the sand, playfully shaking her head from side to side.

This looked fun, but Lily quickly pointed out, "You have large jaws and teeth. I just have a beaky little bill, and I can't possibly pick up those big branches."

Kyppa dropped the branch and sat next to the duckling, "What else can we do?"

Lily smiled and said, "I know, let's go *flyyying*!" As she flapped her little wings she began to soar into the blue sky, circling the beach from above. Kyppa sat and watched, "Hey, Lily! Your wings are wonderful for flying, but I don't have wings!"

The duckling swooped down and landed on Kyppa's back.

The two became discouraged and wondered, if they didn't have anything in common, how could they be friends?

At that moment, Kyppa's ears popped up as she heard a young boy crying out.

"Look," she said. Across the pond, they saw a toddler in a small boat, which was drifting into the pond. This looked unsafe and the pair knew they had to help. Without a word, they took off. Lily took flight and Kyppa ran like the wind.

A worried mom ran from the woods shouting for help. She was too far away to help, but Kyppa was right at the boat.

The duckling shouted from above, "Grab the rope!". With a mighty leap, Kyppa lunged towards the boat, where a rope floated in the shallow water.

Water sloshed into the boat. Although Kyppa was trying to help, this frightened the little boy, and he began to tremble.

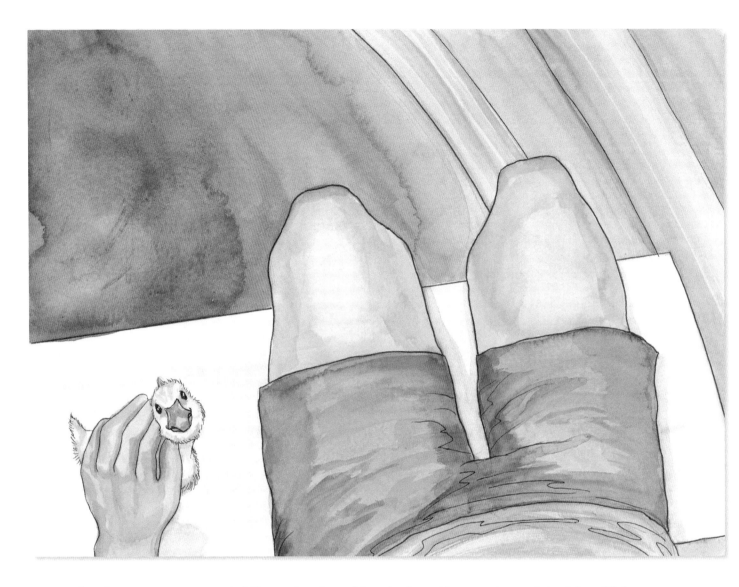

At that very moment, Lily arrived and landed on the seat next to him. This calmed him immediately, and he began to pet the duckling.

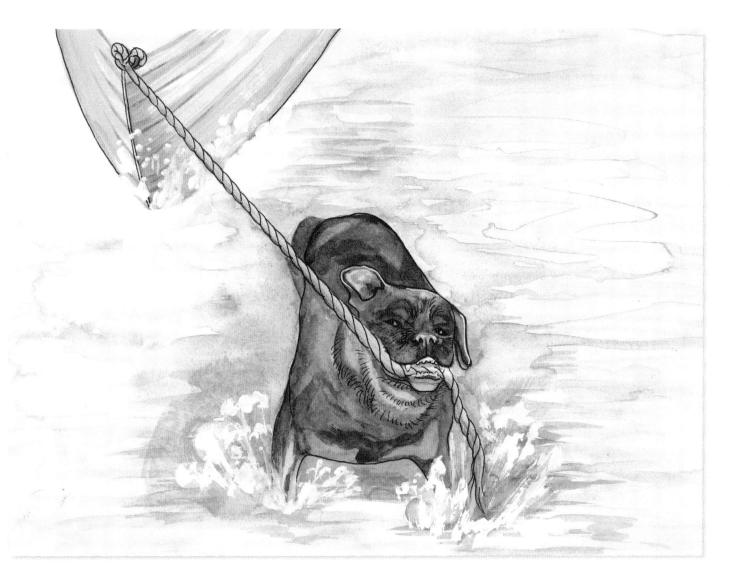

Kyppa then used her strong jaws and legs to *pull* the boat onto shore! They did it!

The little boy jumped onto the sand safely and ran into his mother's arms. She gazed at the dog and the duckling and thanked them with a huge smile.

She knew they were more than a team, they were heroes! Hand-in-hand, mother and son disappeared back down the path into the woods.

Lily looked up at Kyppa and quacked, "Hey, just because we don't have much in common doesn't mean we don't make a great team!"

Kyppa wuffed in response, "We used our own unique strengths to save that boy!" The two grinned at each other with pride.

"Know what I'd like to do now?" said the duckling, "take a *nap*."

"Now, *that's* something we have in common!" and the two curled up cozily for a well-earned snooze!

WITH GRATITUDE

First, thank you to Karyn Kloumann for believing in me and making a 20+ year dream come true. Also, thanks to Shannon Sterner for the beautiful illustrations and capturing my sweet girl's spirit on these pages.

Thank you to my friends and family: Jeff, Chris, Pat, Christine, Lindsay, Steve & Linda, The ELP, The Squire, my JWU Griffins and The Six. I'm blessed to have you in my life and whether we speak once a day, once a month or once a year.... you fill my heart with happiness!

Thank you to Josh, for being by my side, always supportive and understanding. You're the best dad to our four legged kids and I love you always!

Thank you to all the rescues and advocates for your tireless commitment to end suffering, cruelty, abuse or neglect of man's (and woman's) best friend. Your dedication to the helpless inspires me every day.

Thankful for the memories of those I miss dearly, I wish you were here: Mom, Papa, York and Kyppa.

44730625R00020

Made in the USA
Charleston, SC
30 July 2015